Monster
of Disguise

ALSO IN THE JUNIOR MONSTER SCOUTS SERIES

JUNIOR MONSTER SCOUTS

#4 Monster of Disguise

By Joe McGee
Illustrated by Ethan Long

ALADDIN
NEW YORK   LONDON   TORONTO   SYDNEY   NEW DELHI

ALADDIN

An imprint of Simon & Schuster Children's Publishing Division
1230 Avenue of the Americas, New York, New York 10020
First Aladdin hardcover edition September 2020
Text copyright © 2020 by Joseph McGee
Illustrations copyright © 2020 by Ethan Long
Also available in an Aladdin paperback edition.
For information about special discounts for bulk purchases, please contact Simon & Schuster Special Sales at 1-866-506-1949 or business@simonandschuster.com.
The Simon & Schuster Speakers Bureau can bring authors to your live event.
For more information or to book an event contact the Simon & Schuster Speakers Bureau at 1-866-248-3049 or visit our website at www.simonspeakers.com.
Jacket designed by Karin Paprocki
Interior designed by Mike Rosamilia
The illustrations for this book were rendered digitally.
The text of this book was set in Centaur MT.
Manufactured in the United States of America 0720 FFG
2 4 6 8 10 9 7 5 3 1
Library of Congress Control Number 2019955601
ISBN 978-1-5344-3686-2 (hc)
ISBN 978-1-5344-3685-5 (pbk)
ISBN 978-1-5344-3687-9 (eBook)

For that teacher who saw in ten-year-old me
my passion for writing and helped me believe
I could do something with it

★ ★ ★ ★

THANK YOU

· THE SCOUTS ·

VAMPYRA may be a vampire, but that doesn't mean she wants your blood. Gross! In fact, she doesn't even like ketchup! She loves gymnastics, especially cart-wheels, and one of her favorite things is hanging upside down . . . even when she's *not* a bat. She loves garlic in her food and sleeps in past noon, preferring the nighttime over the day. She lives in Castle Dracula with her mom, dad (Dracula), and aunts, who are always after her to brush her fangs and clean her cape.

WOLFY and his family live high in the mountains above Castle Dracula, where they can get the best view of the moon. He likes to hike and play in the creek and gaze at the stars. He especially likes to fetch sticks with his dad, Wolf Man, and go on family pack runs, even if he has to put up with all of his little brothers and sisters. They're always howling when he tries to talk! Mom says he has his father's fur. Boy, is he proud of that!

 FRANKY STEIN has always been bigger than the other monsters. But it's not just his body that's big. It's his brain and his heart as well. He has plenty of hugs and smiles to go around. His dad, Frankenstein, is the scoutmaster, and one of Franky's favorite things is his well-worn Junior Monster Scout handbook. One day Franky is going to be a scoutmaster, like his dad. But for now . . . he wants a puppy. Dad says he'll make Franky one soon. Mom says Franky has to keep his workshop clean for a week first.

GLOOMY
WOODS

LAKE

VILLAGE

BARON VON
GRUMP'S HOUSE

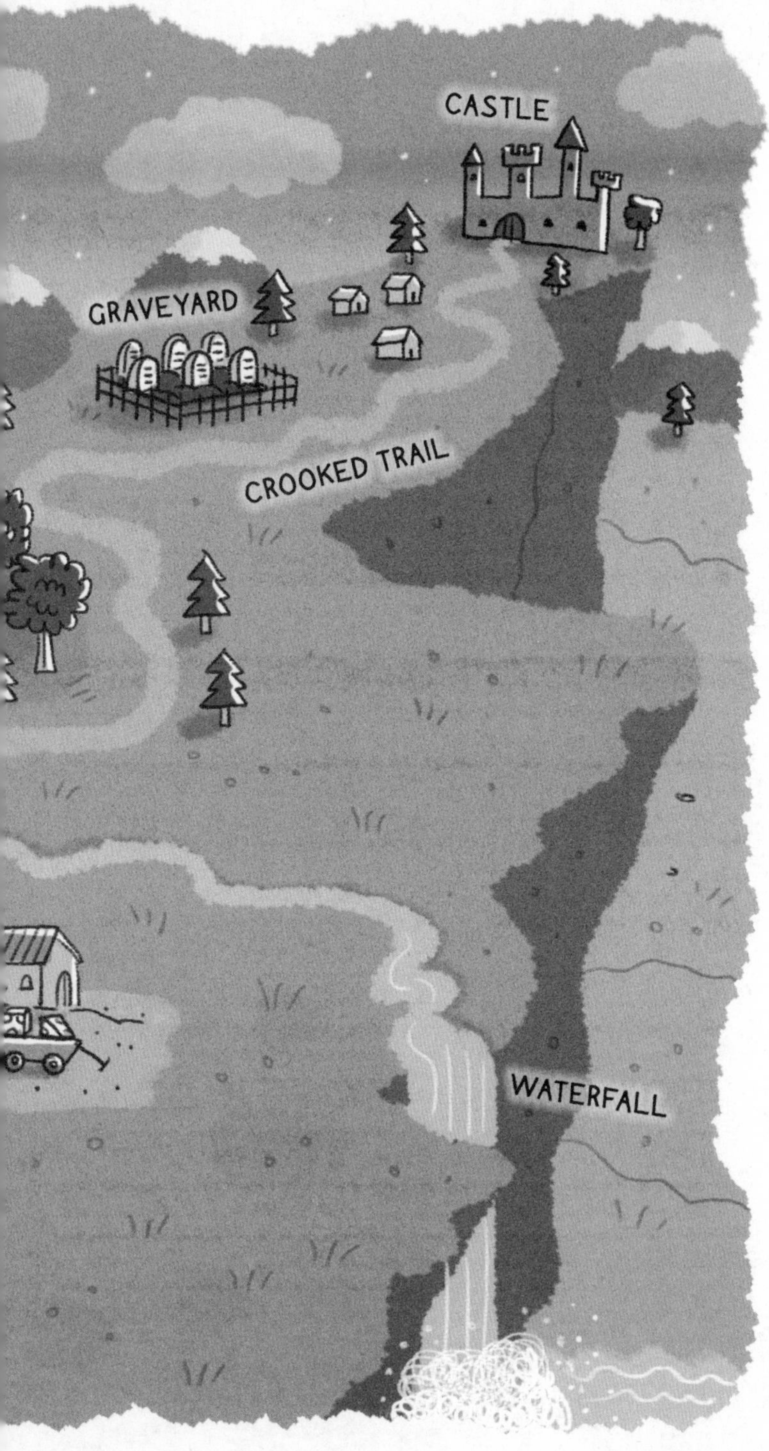
CASTLE
GRAVEYARD
CROOKED TRAIL
WATERFALL

Monster
of Disguise

CHAPTER

1

AH, SUMMER IN THE VILLAGE . . . YOU CAN practically smell the sweet scent of grass and wildflowers. Of horses and hay and freshly baked cookies. The sun is shining. The birds are singing. Boys and girls, young and old, are flying kites. All is well in the village. And why shouldn't it be? So far these villagers have managed to avoid a horde of hungry, cheese-eating rats during their annual cheese festival; celebrate their 150th birthday with only a momentary loss of power; and not get swept away by the flooding river and strong winds during a sudden spring storm.

How did they survive all of these things? I'm glad you asked. Why, the Junior Monster Scouts, of course! Those Junior Monster Scouts are always in the right place at the right time, aren't they? And speaking of Junior Monster Scouts . . . where *are* they?

Let's take a look, shall we?

Wolfy raced ahead of his cub brothers and sisters. Wolfy's dad, Wolf Man, hurled a stick over their heads.

"And . . . fetch!" Wolf Man said.

Fetch was Wolfy's favorite game. He loved running as fast as he could, jump-

ing over logs and rocks and fences, and getting that stick. Dad said he was the fastest!

"No fair!" said Wolfy's little sister Fern. "You always get the stick!"

"One of these days, I'll bet you catch me!" Wolfy said.

The rest of the cubs tumbled around Wolfy's feet, howling and barking.

Meanwhile, way up at the top of the castle tower, Vampyra gazed out her bedroom window.

"Vampyra!" Aunt Belladonna called. "Are you brushing your fangs?"

"You have to keep them shiny and pointy!" said Aunt Hemlock.

"Don't forget to floss!" Aunt Moonflower added.

Vampyra groaned and trudged back to her sink. How many times did she have to brush her fangs?

"Until they're done right!" Aunt Hemlock called up from the library.

"Reading my mind isn't fair!" said Vampyra. She stuck her toothbrush in her mouth and scowled.

Franky put the collar on his new puppy, attached her leash, and wound her up.

"Good girl!" he said. "Want to go for a walk?"

Sprocket wagged her tail. She was very excited.

"Woof!" she said. "Woof! Woof!"

Franky patted her on the head and started down the Crooked Trail. He was so excited to have a new puppy. He and his dad had made her all by themselves in Doctor Frankenstein's laboratory. Even his cousin Igor Junior had helped.

And while Franky and Sprocket walked and whistled down the Crooked Trail, while Wolfy played fetch, while Vampyra brushed her fangs *again*, and while the villagers flew kites and watched clouds, someone else was up and about. Someone with big, black, bushy eyebrows. Someone with a permanent scowl. Someone with the initials B. V. G.

Do you know who it is?

Of course you do. It was none other than Baron Von Grump.

He paced his little balcony, wringing his hands and watching the winding road that led to his crooked windmill.

"Where is it?" he asked. "It should be here this morning."

"Caw?" asked Edgar, his pet crow.

"I'm glad you asked," said Baron Von Grump. He smiled an oily, sneaky smile. The kind of smile a snake might make before it bit you. The kind of smile that makes you think someone is up to no good. "I'm waiting for a very special delivery. I have a little surprise in store for these kite-flying, cloud-gazing villagers. Every single time I try to get some peace and quiet, they have to ruin it with their noisome fun! But not this time. This time I have just the thing. . . ."

He peered down the road. An old truck bounced and clattered toward him.

"Ah! Here it comes now!"

• • •

Oh boy, you and I know that whatever is in that truck is *not* good for the villagers, because nothing involving Baron Von Grump is *ever* good! I suppose we'll have to wait and see what it is.

CHAPTER

2

FRANKY AND SPROCKET HAD ONLY JUST started down the path when Franky's mom, Esmeralda, called out to him.

"Don't forget that we're having a special scout campfire tonight!" she said.

"Oh boy!" said Franky. "Will there be s'mores?"

"S'mores and more!" she said. "But I need you to pick up some chocolate from the village. Those villagers make the best chocolate!"

It's true, you know. Imagine the best piece of chocolate you've ever had. Do you remember how sweet it was? How rich? How absolutely delicious in all of its chocolaty goodness? Now multiply that by a thousand. That's how good the village chocolate was.

Esmeralda gave Franky some money for chocolate and off he went, leash in hand and a smile on his face.

"Wait up, Franky!" said Vampyra. She flittered down from her bedroom window in bat form.

"Vampyra!" called Aunt Belladonna. "Don't forget to pick up the graham crackers for s'mores tonight!"

Vampyra wrapped her bat wings around

herself and spun in a circle. One . . . two . . . three . . . POOF! She turned into herself—shiny, brushed fangs and all.

"Hi, Vampyra!" Franky said.

"Woof!" said Sprocket. She wagged

her tail very fast. She was excited to see Vampyra.

"We're going for a walk," said Franky. "Want to come? I have to get chocolate for s'mores."

"I'm getting graham crackers," said Vampyra.

They had just reached the covered bridge when they met Wolfy. But he was not alone. He had all of his little cub brothers and sisters with him. They chased one another around his feet and nipped at his tail and howled at the sky.

"Hey, Wolfy, do you and your brothers and sisters want to come with us?" asked Vampyra.

"We have to get chocolate and graham

13

crackers for the s'mores tonight," said Franky.

"Me too," said Wolfy. "Mom sent us to get marshmallows . . . and exercise."

The cubs ran in circles. They leaped fallen logs. They climbed atop rocks. They had a lot of energy.

"Woof!" said Sprocket. She wanted the cubs to pet her. And, of course, they did. Who would not want to pet a puppy? A fuzzy, cute, tail-wagging puppy?

Well . . . there is *one* person who would not want to pet a puppy. There is *one* person who would look at your fuzzy, cute, tail-wagging puppy and say, *Bah! Leave me alone.* And right now, he was in his crooked windmill, opening his special delivery. . . .

• • •

"Behold!" said Baron Von Grump as he pried open the lid of the large wooden crate. "The very thing I've been waiting for!"

"Caw?" asked Edgar.

"Yes, Edgar, it is a mirror. But not just *any* mirror. This, my feathered friend, is the amazing, wondrous, spectacular, super-duper HypnoMirror! Just by gazing into this mirror, you will be hypnotized and under my control!"

Edgar covered his eyes with his wings and looked away.

"Don't worry," said Baron Von Grump. "It's not on . . . yet." And then he smiled that poisonous-snake smile, just like before.

But back in the village, things were much different. The villagers were flying kites and watching clouds and riding unicycles back and forth. There was accordion music and fresh flowers and the sweet smell of delicious chocolate.

The Junior Monster Scouts, along with Sprocket and the cubs, crossed over the covered bridge and into the village.

"I can't wait for s'mores tonight," said Vampyra. "Even if it means I have to brush my fangs a hundred more times."

"I wish I could have s'mores."

"You are," said Vampyra. She looked at Franky. "We're having them tonight, at our scout campfire, remember?"

"I didn't say anything," said Franky.

"A campfire? That sounds fun!"

"Wolfy, did you forget already?" Franky asked. "You know we're having a campfire. You're supposed to get the marshmallows for the s'mores."

"Of course I know," said Wolfy. "I didn't say that."

"Then who did?" asked Vampyra.

"Me."

"Me who?" asked Wolfy.

"Me who, who?"

"Are you an owl?" Franky asked, looking up at the tops of the buildings.

"No," said the voice. "I'm a boy. I'm right here!"

Franky, Wolfy, Vampyra, Sprocket, and the cubs all looked at where the voice was coming from.

But there was nobody there.

WHEN SOMEONE SAYS, "I'M RIGHT HERE!" and you look and there is nobody there, that can be very confusing. You might think that there is something wrong with your eyes. Or maybe that you are hearing things. Or maybe even that someone is playing a prank on you. That's exactly what the Junior Monster Scouts thought. They thought that someone was trying to play a funny trick on them.

"Peter, is that you?" asked Franky. Peter,

the piper, was a friend of the Junior Monster Scouts. They had helped him find his cat, Shadow, when she was lost in the Gloomy Woods.

"Who's Peter?" the voice asked.

"*Who* said that?" asked Wolfy.

"Where are you?" asked Vampyra. "Come out and show yourself. Stop playing tricks!"

"I'm right *here*," the voice said. "I told you guys . . ."

"Wolfy, look!" said Fern, the littlest of the little wolf cubs. She pointed to where a rock floated up off the ground and stopped. It hung in midair all by itself.

But . . . it *wasn't* all by itself. There was a hand holding it. An invisible hand that belonged to an invisible boy. Because it was invisible, nobody could see it. I'll give you an example. I'm going to tell you how this story ends, but I'm going to write it in invisible ink. Ready? Okay, just read the next line and you'll know how the story ends:

Well, what do you think? Good ending, right? Were you surprised? Wait . . . what? You couldn't read it? No, of course you couldn't read it. It was invisible. And that is exactly what the Junior Monster Scouts saw when they looked at where the rock was floating . . . nothing.

"Whoa," said Wolfy. "That rock is talk-ing!"

"It's not the rock, it's me," said the voice. "I'm invisible!"

"That explains why we can't see you," said Franky.

"That's the problem," said the voice. "Nobody can see me. I'm just an invisible boy."

"What's your name?" asked Vampyra.

"George," said the invisible boy. "Hey, can I pet your dog?"

"You sure can, George," said Franky. "Hey, she likes you!"

Sure enough, Sprocket wagged her tail and licked the space where George must have been standing. To everyone else, it looked like she was licking the air.

"I guess that answers my question as

to why I've never seen you in the village before," Vampyra said.

"What does?" asked George.

"Being invisible," she said.

"Oh no," said George, "I don't live here. I've only just arrived. I was hoping that maybe *someone* might see me."

"It must be tough when nobody can see you," Wolfy said.

"And lonely," said George.

"My brother is a Junior Monster Scout," said Fern. She stood as tall as she could (which was not very tall at all, but she tried). "He'll help you!"

"You will?" George asked.

"Of course," said Wolfy. "We all will. That's what we do!"

"And you can even come to our camp-fire tonight," said Vampyra. "We're having s'mores!"

"Wow, thanks, Junior Monster Scouts," George said.

But the scouts did not get a chance to say "you're welcome" (which is a very nice thing to say when someone says "thanks"). Because at that moment, a very large, very colorful wagon pulled by four very large horses bounced its way up the road. It was not the wagon, or the horses, that interrupted their conversation. It was the man driving the large, colorful wagon, and his equally colorful cape and silly glasses and tall top hat.

"Gather round, gather round," he said,

riding his large, colorful wagon right into the middle of the village. "Stop flying your kites. Stop gazing at clouds. Put down your unicycles and gather around. Step right up, step right up, to my Fun House of . . . FUN!"

The village mayor stopped his unicycle and clapped his hands. "Ooh, that *does* sound fun!" he said.

A Fun House of Fun seems pretty awesome, doesn't it? But if the mayor had looked closer, he might have suspected that it was not going to be as fun as it sounded. If he had looked past the colorful cape, or the tall top hat, or the swirly glasses, or the striped scarf, he might have seen that the man driving this Fun House of Fun was none other than Baron

Von Grump! And Baron Von Grump is not so fun.

And had the mayor looked even closer, he might have seen a few black feathers sticking out from under that tall top hat. But he did not. Nobody did, because, well . . . Fun House of *FUN*!

"And now, simple villagers," said the top hat–wearing, cape-swirling villain in disguise, "who will be the first to step right up and have some *FUN*?" He pulled out a cane from somewhere inside of his cape, twirled it around, and pointed it at the Junior Monster Scouts. "What about you, Junior Monster Scouts?" he sneered.

But before they could answer, the mayor raised his hand. "Ooh, ooh, pick me!" he said. "I want to go first. After all, I *am* the mayor!"

Baron Von Grump smiled a crooked smile and pulled down the steps to the large wagon.

"Well then," he said, "prepare for the most fun you have ever had!"

The mayor practically skipped up the steps and opened the door to the wagon.

"Fun, here I come!" he said.

4

WHEN THE MAYOR STEPPED INTO THE wagon, he was not disappointed. The walls of the wagon were painted a very fun color. There were polka dots and stripes and swirls and splatters of rainbow colors. The floor was covered in a very fun rug. It was fuzzy and warm and had plenty of pleasing patterns. There was also some very fun music playing from a little turntable in the corner. It was the kind of music that makes you want to tap your toes and snap your fingers and bob your head to the funky beat. And while all of these things were certainly fun, what really made the Fun House of Fun *especially* fun was the peculiar mirror standing in the very center of the wagon.

The mayor stood before the mirror and made silly faces. He stuck out his tongue. He rolled his eyes. He pulled on his mustache.

"Oh my," he said, "this certainly *is* fun!"

But then something strange happened. Something very out of the ordinary. A large swirl formed in the middle of the mirror. It was a black-and-white swirl that began to spin, faster and faster and faster. The mayor could not look away.

And then something even stranger happened. The mayor's eyes had the exact same swirl. He was hypnotized! His swirly eyes stared straight ahead, and he shuffled out the door on the other side of the wagon.

"How was it, Mayor?" asked one villager.

"Fun," he said.

"On a scale from one to ten, how fun was it?" asked another villager.

"Fun," said the mayor.

"That sounds like the most fun ever!" said a third villager. "I'm going to buy a hundred tickets!"

"So. Much. Fun," said the mayor.

"That's right, ladies and gentle-villagers!" said the disguised Baron Von Grump. "Step right up and get your tickets here! The one and only Fun House of Fun!"

The villagers lined up, waving their money in the air. They could not wait to enter the Fun House of Fun. Why, the mayor himself had said it was So. Much. Fun.

"I'll take one," said a villager, waving her money at Baron Von Grump.

"I'll take three," said another villager, shoving his money into Baron Von Grump's hands.

"Fifteen for me!" said a third, pushing a wheelbarrow of money right up to the wagon.

"I'll have this mirror paid off in no time," Baron Von Grump whispered to Edgar.

"Caw?" asked Edgar.

"Oh yes, very expensive," said Baron Von Grump. "Terribly expensive. But it'll be worth every penny once I have them all under my control." Baron Von Grump snickered. "These villagers don't even know that they're paying for their own hypnosis!"

Baron Von Grump could not hand out tickets fast enough. Even Edgar couldn't keep up. As Baron Von Grump took the villagers' money, he handed it up to Edgar, who stashed it all under the baron's tall top hat. And as Edgar stashed the money in the tall top hat, the baron handed each villager a ticket. It read:

ADMIT ONE
FUN HOUSE OF FUN
- NO REFUNDS -

The line stretched from one end of the village to the other. Everyone wanted to have as much fun as the mayor had had. Nobody wanted to miss out. Not even Wolfy's little brothers and sisters.

"Can we go in?" asked little Fern. "Please?"

Wolfy scratched his head. He was supposed to use his money to buy marshmallows.

"Pretty puhleazzeeeee," said Fern. The

other cubs all joined in, howling and pulling at Wolfy's tail.

"Woof! Woof!" said Sprocket.

"I think Sprocket wants to go in too," Franky said.

"But if I buy tickets for all of the cubs, how am I supposed to buy the marshmallows for s'mores?" asked Wolfy.

"I think I can help," said George. "Since you invited me for s'mores tonight, I ought to bring something. What if I bring marshmallows? And then you can use your money to buy tickets!"

"That's a great idea," Wolfy said.

"Thank you, George!" said Fern and the rest of the cubs. Fern would have hugged him, but she did not know exactly where he was standing. Being invisible made it very hard for George to be hugged.

In fact, you should stop reading for a second and hug someone you *can* see.

I'll wait. . . .

Done? Hug delivered? Okay, good. Now, where were we?

Ah, yes . . . the tickets . . .

5

WOLFY STEPPED RIGHT UP TO THE MAN in the tall top hat, just like the man instructed. The man was saying, "Step right up! Step right up!" And people were! All of the villagers were stepping right up and handing the man in the tall top hat their money in exchange for a ticket into the Fun House of Fun.

"You look familiar," said Wolfy. "Do I know you?"

"Why, um . . . NO," said the man in the tall top hat (who you and I know was really Baron Von Grump in disguise). "Of course you don't. Why would you? I've never been to this village before. I don't know anything about that crooked Old Windmill, and I certainly don't live there. I'm just a simple traveler, bringing fun wherever I go. I am not up to any kind of sneaky trick, and I am certainly not wearing a disguise!"

He grinned a very toothy grin.

Wolfy shrugged. "Okay. In that case, let me have . . ." He turned to count everyone. "One, two, three . . . eleven tickets."

"But I only see ten of you," said the baron.

"That's because our friend George is invisible," said Wolfy.

"Invisible?" asked the baron. "I don't believe you."

"He's standing right there," said Wolfy. He pointed to an empty spot next to Vampyra.

"Raise your hand, invisible boy," said Baron Von Grump.

Edgar crawled out from under the top hat and peered at the spot. He didn't see anything.

"Caw!" said Edgar.

"I didn't see anyone raise a hand either," said Baron Von Grump.

"That's because he's invisible!" Franky said.

"See?" George said. "Nobody ever notices me."

"Who said that!?" asked Baron Von Grump.

"George did," said Vampyra. "We told you, he's *invisible*."

Baron Von Grump squinted one eye. He squinted the other. He peered at them very closely. He did not trust monsters, and he certainly did not trust the Junior Monster *Scouts*.

"I'm watching you," he said. "Don't think you can pull any funny tricks on me. In you go!"

Wolfy and the cubs were the first to go in.

"Wow, look at those walls!" said Wolfy. "This *is* fun!"

"Check out this warm, fuzzy rug!" Fern said.

"I like the music!" said another of the cubs.

"Look at this *mirror*!" said another cub.

As soon as Wolfy and the cubs were inside, the door shut behind them.

When they came out the other side, they were acting very odd.

"How was it?" asked Vampyra.

"Yeah, was it *super* fun?" Franky asked.

"It must have been SO much fun that they can't even describe it!" said George.

Wolfy and the cubs did not respond at all. It was like they were in a trance. They just stared into the clouds, and their eyes were quite strange, like swirling spirals going around and around.

"Hey, look," said Vampyra. "There's Peter. Maybe he can tell us how much fun it is."

"Peter, over here!" Franky said.

But Peter didn't answer them either. He didn't even seem to notice them. And when Franky and Vampyra looked at his eyes, they saw the same swirling spiral going around and around and around.

"I don't like this," said Vampyra.

"Something's not right," Franky said.

"Vampyra? Franky?" said George. "Look!"

They didn't have to see where he was pointing with his invisible hand to know what he was talking about.

Everyone was standing in the center of the village . . .

. . . staring at nothing with their swirling spiral eyes!

6

NOW, IF YOU SAW ALL OF YOUR FRIENDS and family staring at nothing, with swirling spiral eyes, you would probably suspect that something was not right. Something was not right at all. This was exactly what Vampyra, Franky, and George thought.

No matter how much they talked to them, no matter how many times they waved their hands in front of their eyes, no matter how many silly faces or goofy noises they made, nobody would even look in their direction. Not the villagers, not Peter, not even Wolfy or the cubs.

"It's like we're invisible," said Vampyra.

"Now you know how I feel," said George.

"Woof," said Sprocket. She licked George's invisible hand.

But then something even stranger happened.

The man in the tall top hat stood before the hypnotized crowd of villagers (and Wolfy and the cubs). He placed a small platform on the ground. He stepped up onto the small platform.

"Now that I have enough of you—"

"Caw," said Edgar.

"Well, *most* of you—"

"Caw, caw."

"Oh. Really? Well, that's even better than expected," said the man in the tall top hat to the crow sitting next to him. He turned back to the motionless villagers. "Now that I have *all* of you, it's time for a little test. Cluck like a chicken!"

The mayor, Peter, the villagers, and Wolfy and the cubs all began to cluck like chickens.

"Cluck, cluck, cluck," they all said, wiggling their arms like chickens and strutting around in circles with their heads bobbing back and forth.

It was a very funny sight to see, and Franky, Vampyra, and George wanted to laugh, but they didn't. They knew that this

top hat–wearing Fun House owner was very suspicious.

"Well, they certainly *seem* to be hypnotized," said the man in the tall top hat.

"Caw, caw, caw."

"Yes, of course, it never hurts to be sure,"

said the man in the tall top hat. "Now moo like a cow!"

As you might have guessed, all of the villagers, and the mayor, and Peter, and Wolfy and the cubs began mooing like cows. Again, it was a funny sight, but the Junior Monster Scouts were not laughing. They were very worried.

"What are they doing?" asked Vampyra.

"They're mooing," said Franky. "Like cows."

"I *know* that," said Vampyra. "I mean *why* are they mooing like cows?"

"I think they're . . . hypnotized," said George.

"Hypno-*what*?" Vampyra asked.

"You know, hypnotized," said George. "Like in a trance."

"But what could have possibly hypno-tized them?" Franky asked.

"Well, let's retrace our steps," said Vampyra. "You know, like what you do when something is lost."

"Let's start with Wolfy and the cubs," said George, "since we know everything they did before becoming hypnotized."

"They came to the village with us," said Vampyra.

"They bought tickets for the Fun House of Fun," said Franky.

"Then they went inside the Fun House of Fun," said George.

"And when they came out . . . they were hypno-sized," said Vampyra.

"Hypno*tized*," said George.

"That's what I said," Vampyra said.

"Aha!" said Franky. "Hypno-sized, hypno-tized . . . whatever it is, it must have something to do with the Fun House of Fun," said Franky.

"I'll bet you're right," said Vampyra. "They were normal when they went **in** and then *not* normal when they came **out**."

"There's only one way to know," said George.

"One of us is going to have to go in and check it out," said Franky.

"Not one," Vampyra said. "All of us." She put her hand out. "A Junior Monster Scout and friends . . ."

Franky put his hand on top of hers.

". . . stick together till the end," he finished.

An invisible hand rested atop Franky's and Vampyra's hands.

CHAPTER
7

WHILE THE MAN IN THE TALL TOP HAT and his crow assistant performed their final test to be absolutely certain the villagers were under their complete control, Franky, Vampyra, and George were putting their tickets to use.

"Time for a little detective work," said Vampyra.

Franky opened his Junior Monster Scout

handbook and turned to the list of merit badges. "You know," he said, "I'll bet we can even get our Mystery Merit Badges if we solve this case."

"I think you're right," said Vampyra. "This sure sounds like a mystery to me!"

Franky, Vampyra, and George placed their tickets in the ticket box and climbed up the steps and through the door of the Fun House of Fun. Sprocket waited outside.

The inside was, as you and I know, very fun. There was fun music playing, fun rugs on the ground, fun paint on the walls, and a very, *very* fun mirror right in the middle of the room.

"Haha," said Franky. "I look super tall. The mirror stretched me out!"

"Look at me," said Vampyra. "I look shorter and kind of flat!"

"Aw, rats," said George. "I don't see anything at all."

"Did someone say 'rats'?" said a very large rat, gnawing on a hunk of cheese.

That was Boris, and he lived in the basement of Castle Dracula with all of the other rats. They were always sticking their cheese-covered noses into everyone's business. Boris was not alone. There were several other rats with him.

But it was a good thing that Boris and the rats *did* stick their cheese-covered noses into this business because just as the Junior Monster Scouts were staring at the mirror, their eyes began to turn swirly and spiral and lose all focus. . . .

"Hey! Junior Monster Scouts," said Boris
the rat. "We're talking to you. Over here!
Wow . . . that's a *fun* mirror!"

Vampyra, Franky, and George heard Boris
and turned from the mirror just in time.

"Boris, what are you doing here?" asked Vampyra.

"Hey, look at their eyes!" Franky said.

"They're swirly spirals, just like everyone's outside!" George said

Sure enough, Boris and the rats weren't eating their cheese anymore, and Boris didn't answer Vampyra's question. It wasn't because they were being rude—it was because they were hypnotized!

Have you ever been hypnotized? No? I want you to do something. On the count of three, I want you to quack like a duck. Do you know how to quack like a duck? I'll bet you do. Okay, ready? One . . . two . . . three!

Ah, very good. But guess what? I just

hypnotized you! I made you quack like a
duck. That was exactly what was happen-
ing to Boris and the rats, and Wolfy and
the cubs, and Peter, the mayor, the villagers . . . Wow, that is a lot of quacking and

mooing and clucking and barking. That is a lot of noise.

And do you know who doesn't like noise?

Baron Von Grump.

Which is why, at that exact moment, he made everyone *stop* making animal noises. No more quacking. No more mooing. No more clucking or barking. He made everyone be quiet.

"Silence!" he said.

Everyone was absolutely silent.

He took off his tall top hat and removed the rest of his disguise.

"Ah, do you hear that, Edgar?" he asked.

"Caw?" Edgar asked.

"Exactly," said Baron Von Grump. "There's nothing to hear. Nothing! Because finally,

the day has come. Finally, the villagers are quiet. No gum chewing, no smiling, no accordions or 'Hello, how do you do?' No walking, no talking, no singing or kite flying. Absolute silence.

"This," said Baron Von Grump, "is the moment I've been waiting for."

He closed his eyes and smiled.

It was an awkward smile. Like maybe a quarter of a smile. He really wasn't any good at smiling, but hey, he tried.

"Edgar?"

"Caw?"

"Breathe quieter."

CHAPTER

8

INSIDE THE FUN HOUSE OF FUN, THE Junior Monster Scouts and George had just discovered something. Something very important. Something that could help them solve this mystery.

"I think it has something to do with the mirror," said Franky.

"When I was looking at the mirror, I began to feel a little sleepy," said Vampyra.

"Me too," said Franky.

"I didn't feel a thing," said George. "This place really isn't that fun. I couldn't even see myself in the mirror."

"And when Boris and the rats looked in the mirror, *they* became hypno-sized!" Vampyra said.

"Hypno*tized*," said George.

"That's what I said."

"That's it!" said Franky. "When someone sees themself in the mirror, they become hypnotized."

"Just like Boris and the rats," said Vampyra. "Hey, where are they going?"

Boris and the rats all walked in a quiet single-file line, right through the other door and out of the Fun House of Fun. They weren't even eating their cheese. That's how quiet they were being!

"Come on," said Vampyra. "Let's follow them!"

Franky, Vampyra, and George followed Boris and the rats. They followed them right to the center of the village, where everyone stood in a trance, watching someone sitting atop a hay wagon.

That someone was enjoying every second of his newly created silence.

That someone was Baron Von Grump.

"Oh, what a glorious day," he said. "Oh, wonderful, magnificent, *quiet* day!"

"It's Baron Von Grump!" said Vampyra.

"Caw?" asked Edgar, turning in their direction.

Franky and Vampyra ducked. George did not duck in time.

But as you might have guessed, Edgar did not see him.

"It's nothing," said Baron Von Grump. "There's no one there. See?" He pointed in their direction, and sure enough, there was nobody to be seen.

Edgar shrugged.

The Junior Monster Scouts breathed a sigh of relief.

George had an idea.

9

GEORGE'S IDEA WAS A VERY GOOD IDEA.
He and the Junior Monster Scouts had figured out that the mirror had something to
do with everyone being hypnotized. They
also knew that only Franky and Vampyra
could see their reflections in the mirror,
which meant . . .

"If I can't see myself in the mirror, and
nobody else can see me, then I'll bet I won't
get hypnotized!" said George.

"You're right!" Franky said.

"Brilliant!" said Vampyra. "Don't worry, Wolfy. Don't worry, cubs. We're going to unhypno-size you!"

But Wolfy and the cubs did not respond.

George did not bother to try to correct her this time. "I thought vampires couldn't see their reflections in the mirror," he said.

Vampyra shrugged. "That's just another made-up story. Okay, what now?"

"Follow me," said George.

"George?" said Vampyra.

"Yes?"

"We can't."

"Oh, right," he said. "Invisible. You go inside first."

Vampyra went first. Then Franky. He told Sprocket to wait outside.

"Bark twice if anyone comes, okay?"

Sprocket wagged her tail and sat by the door. She was a very good watchdog.

George followed them inside the Fun House of Fun and shut the door.

"Now what?" asked Vampyra. She was very careful to keep her eyes off the mirror.

"We need something to cover the mirror with," said George.

Franky had an idea. He reached outside and snatched Baron Von Grump's cape from the hook on the wagon.

"We can use this," he said. He was also very careful to keep his eyes off the mirror.

"Good thinking!" said George.

"Okay, George," said Vampyra. "Cover that mirror!"

George stood in front of the mirror. He looked right into it. All he saw was a cape, floating in the air. George stepped closer and covered the mirror with the cape.

Outside, Baron Von Grump sat atop a mound of hay, in the back of a wagon, in the center of the village, in complete and utter silence. He closed his eyes.

He took a deep breath. It . . . was . . . perfect.

"Caw?" Edgar asked.

Baron Von Grump glowered at Edgar.

"I don't know where those other monsters are, and I don't care," he said. "Can't you see I finally have my moment of silence?"

"Caw," said Edgar. He pointed back to the Fun House of Fun.

"Yes, yes, they may be in the Fun House of Fun. But who cares? They'll be hypnotized just like everyone else!"

Edgar shrugged.

"Now, silence!" said Baron Von Grump.

He closed his eyes. He took a deep breath. He listened to . . . nothing.

Silence

Shhhhh . . . .

Quiet zone

No talking

This means you!

Don't read this aloud.

Too late . . . You're already doing it?

Well, stop.

What do you mean you can't stop?

Do you *have* to read the words on the page?

What do you mean,

"That's what the words on the page are for"?

Fine, be that way.

10

"LOOK, THERE'S A LEVER," SAID FRANKY.

Vampyra groaned. "Oh no, not another lever," she said.

Vampyra, Franky, and Wolfy had had a very scary experience with a lever in Doctor Frankenstein's laboratory when they'd helped their friend Igor Junior get out of trouble.

"I think this one is okay," Franky said.

"How do you know it's okay?" Vampyra asked.

"It could do anything!" said George.

"There has to be a way to turn it on and off, right?" Franky asked.

"And there doesn't appear to be any other buttons, switches, or levers," said George.

"Wait . . . there's writing," said Franky.

"What's it say?" asked Vampyra.

Franky peered closer. "It says . . ."

HYPNOTIZE

OFF

REVERSE

"So all we have to do is move the lever to reverse," said George.

"Here goes nothing," Franky said.

He pulled the lever.

Baron Von Grump had just settled into a calm, quiet, relaxed moment of silence when . . .

"Woof!" said Sprocket.

Baron Von Grump jumped. He was not expecting Sprocket to bark, and it startled him. But Sprocket was not barking to startle him. She was barking because Wolfy and the cubs had snapped out of their hypnosis. Their eyes weren't spirals or swirly. They seemed very confused. Everyone seemed very confused.

"Sprocket!" Wolfy said. "Where're Franky and Vampyra? Wait a minute. . . . Baron Von Grump?"

"What's going on here?" asked the mayor.

"Why are we all out here around this wagon?" asked another villager.

"Say, what are you doing up there on my hay?" asked a third villager.

"I can explain!" said Baron Von Grump. "It . . . It wasn't me. It was . . ."

"Caw!" said Edgar. "Caw! Caw!"

"Yes, exactly. It was another guy with a very tall top hat, and funny glasses, and a colorful scarf. He hypnotized you! I was just trying to break the spell!"

Wolfy sniffed the air. It smelled like Baron Von Grump was not telling the truth.

"You mean this very tall top hat?" Fern asked. She and the other cubs appeared from behind the ticket stand carrying one very tall top hat.

"And *this* colorful scarf?" asked another cub.

"And these funny glasses?" asked a third cub.

"How did those get there?" asked Baron Von Grump. "Haha . . . that's strange, isn't it?"

"Not as strange as that mirror inside the Fun House of Fun," said a voice right next to Baron Von Grump.

"Who said that?" asked Baron Von Grump.

You and I and Wolfy and the cubs know who said it, but nobody else did because they could not see him. But George had climbed right up next to Baron Von Grump.

"Who said what?" George asked.

"Who's talking?" asked Baron Von Grump. "Who's playing tricks on me?"

"You mean tricks like . . . *hypno-sizing people?*" asked Vampyra. She flittered over to the wagon in her bat form.

"And making them cluck like chickens and moo like cows?" Franky asked. He carried the large, cape-covered mirror out of the Fun House of Fun and set it down.

"Explain yourself," said the mayor.

"I want my money back!" said a villager.

"Get off my hay!" said another villager.

"You wouldn't happen to have any cheese, would you?" Boris asked.

"Caw!" said Edgar.

"Yes!" said Baron Von Grump. "Run!"

He jumped down from the hay wagon and ran as fast as he could toward the Old Windmill. Edgar flapped along above him.

"You can't stop Baron Von Grump forever, you meddling monsters!" he hollered.

"I think your village may have seen the last of him for a bit," said a floating tall top hat and a pair of funny glasses.

"Oh my!" said the mayor. "A talking top hat!"

"George!" Vampyra said. "We can really see you now! Kind of."

"Oh yeah?" he said. "Well, check this out. . . ."

He pulled the cape off the mirror.

Everyone gasped and closed their eyes tight.

11

"IT'S OKAY," GEORGE SAID. "YOU CAN open your eyes."

When the Junior Monster Scouts and the villagers opened their eyes, they saw an ordinary mirror. And standing in front of the mirror was *not* an ordinary sight.

"That cape is floating!" said a villager.

"Just like those silly glasses!" said another.

"And that very tall top hat!" a third villager said.

"No, they're not," said Vampyra. "George is wearing them."

"Who's George?" the mayor asked.

"He's our friend," said Franky.

"He's indivisible," said Fern.

"She means *invisible*," Wolfy said.

Fern shrugged. "That's what I said."

George was very pleased that everyone could, kind of, finally see him. It was nice to be noticed for once.

"George helped us turn off Baron Von Grump's hypnotic mirror," Vampyra said.

"If it weren't for George's help, we might all be hypnotized still," said Franky.

"Moo!" Wolfy said.

Everyone laughed.

"Well," said the mayor, "I think we can find you a better set of clothes than a cape and a very tall top hat. Come with me, young George."

"Where are we going?" George asked.

"Why, to the tailor, of course," said the mayor. "We'll have you dressed in a whole new outfit so that wherever you go in the village, people can stop and say, 'Good morning, George!' and 'How do you do?'"

If Baron Von Grump had heard that, he would have had a fit. Another person in the village to go around saying "good morning"? He would not like that at all.

Speaking of Baron Von Grump . . .

CHAPTER

12

BARON VON GRUMP FUMED. HE FUSSED. He tugged his beard and pounded his fists.

"It was all so perfect!" he said. "It was all going according to plan!"

"Caw! Caw! Caw!" Edgar said.

"Well, how was I to know that those Junior Monster Scouts had an invisible friend? Whose side are you on, anyway?"

Edgar crossed his wings and shook his

head. Sometimes living with Baron Von Grump was a very trying experience. Okay, most of the time. All right, probably *all* of the time.

Just then, there was a knock at the front door.

13

WHILE GEORGE WAS GETTING FITTED at the tailor's, the Junior Monster Scouts busied themselves getting everything they needed for the s'mores. Franky bought the chocolate. Vampyra bought the graham crackers. All they needed were the marsh-mallows.

"Hi, Junior Monster Scouts!" George said.

"Hi, George!" they replied. They could see him now because he was dressed in a whole new outfit. He had a pair of buckled shoes and knee-high socks, pants and a shirt, gloves and glasses, and even a fancy cap on his head. A fancy cap with a feather! The only things they could not see were his mouth and nose.

"I never thought that new clothes might make a difference," he said. "My old clothes must have turned invisible in the same experiment that first turned *me* invisible."

He was also holding a bag of marshmallows.

"Brought you these," he said.

"Now we can have s'mores tonight!" said Fern.

The other cubs all howled with delight.

Sprocket barked and howled along with them.

"Ah, there you are," said the mayor. "George, you are looking splendid. Simply magnificent! I want to show you all something."

The mayor led them to the village square where Peter, the piper, stood next to something tall and rectangular and covered with a sheet.

Peter pulled the sheet off to reveal a full-length mirror. Only, when you looked at it, you did not get hypnotized. Instead, it made you look squashed and extra wide, or stretched out and super skinny, or wavy and wobbly. It was a new fun-house mirror, and this one was actually FUN!

"Junior Monster Scouts, George," said the mayor, "you taught us all another valuable lesson today. It's not what you look like—it's what you *do*. We used to be scared of the monsters because they looked different, but they always come to our aid. And George, you weren't noticed because of what you looked like . . . or *didn't* look like . . . but because you helped save us all from being hypnotized!"

"So what's the mirror for?" asked Wolfy. He stuck his tongue out, and his reflection looked even sillier. His tongue looked ten times as long!

"Because when we look into it," Peter said, "we're reminded that things aren't really what they seem! Even if it *looks* that way."

"But where did that hypnotizing mirror go?" Franky asked.

"You know," said the mayor, "I really don't have the slightest idea."

14

REMEMBER THAT KNOCK AT THE FRONT door of the Old Windmill?

"I'm coming!" hollered Baron Von Grump. "Quit pounding on my door! Noise, noise, noise, NOISE. Always with the noise. What do you—"

"Hey, Von Grump," said Boris the rat. "You left this back at the village. Figured you might want it back."

Baron Von Grump's eyes got very wide.

The rats had brought him back his mirror. His hypnotic mirror.

And they'd just pushed the lever to HYPNOTIZE.

Baron Von Grump's eyes became spirals. Then they got swirly. He was very sleepy.

"Cluck like a chicken," said Boris.

"Cluck! Cluck!" said Baron Von Grump.

"Oink like a pig," said another rat.

"Oink, oink, oink!" Baron Von Grump said.

"Come on," said Boris, leading the rats into the Old Windmill, "let's grab some cheese and sit back and watch the show!"

"Oink, oink, oink!" said Baron Von Grump.

Edgar covered his ears with his wings. Baron Von Grump was SO *noisy*!

CHAPTER
15

THAT NIGHT'S SCOUT MEETING TOOK place around a nice, toasty campfire. Can you smell the wood burning? Can you hear the crackle? Can you see the bright embers dancing up into the star-filled summer sky? Campfires are nice. Summer campfires are even nicer. And summer campfires with s'mores? The best.

"Well, sounds like you had a very exciting afternoon," said Esmeralda. She handed out marshmallow sticks. There were a lot of sticks. Not only were the Junior Monster Scouts there; and their moms; and Vampyra's aunts Belladonna, Hemlock, and Moonflower; but also Dracula, and Wolf Man, and Doctor Frankenstein, and the cubs, and Sprocket, and Igor Junior, and Igor Senior, and finally, last but certainly not least, George.

Wolfy's mom, Harriet, opened her Junior Monster Scout handbook. "Let's start tonight's meeting by saying the scout oath," she said. Everyone joined in.

"*I promise to be nice, not scary. To help, not harm. To always try to do my best. I am a monster, but I am not mean. I am a Junior Monster Scout!*"

"It sounds like you weren't only helpful

today," said Vampyra's mom, Vampirella. "It sounds like you were clever."

"Regular detectives!" said Aunt Belladonna.

"Supersleuths!" said Aunt Hemlock.

"No clue too confusing for these clever monsters!" Aunt Moonflower said.

"Which is why you are receiving your Mystery Merit Badges," said Harriet. "All four of you."

She looked right at George and pinned the merit badge to his shirt.

George smiled, and even though no one could *see* his smile, they could *feel* it.

"Gee, thanks!" he said.

"You're very welcome," said Esmeralda.

"I believe we have another surprise tonight, don't we?" said Dracula.

Vampirella smiled. Her fangs glinted in the campfire light.

"Indeed we do," she said. "Fern, cubs, congratulations. You are the very first *Little Junior Monster Scouts!*"

Wolfy leaped up and howled at the moon. Everyone howled along with him.

It was a Junior Monster Scout meeting to remember!

OINK!

CLUCK!

MOO!

· ACKNOWLEDGMENTS ·

Wow . . . here we are, at the end of the fourth book in the Junior Monster Scouts series. It goes without saying that I want to thank my amazing wife, Jess (not that I have other wives, but I thought it'd be nice to mention her name and not just call her "my wife," and if I'd thanked "Jess," you might have asked, "Who's Jess?"), for her love, support, encouragement, inspiration, and friendship. I want to thank my editor, Karen Nagel, for opening this door to me in the first place and for championing these books. Karen, you and the Aladdin team made these books even greater than I could have ever imagined them. Chelsea

Morgan, thanks for putting up with my habitual mistake with a certain dialogue tag. Thank you, Linda Epstein, for all of the hard work you have done (and continue to do) with this series. Thank you, Ethan, for your wonderful illustrations. I'm a lucky author to be partnered with you.

Shane, Zach, Logan, Ainsley, Sawyer, and Braeden—thank you for being proud of what we do. We are proud of each one of you. And by "we" I am, of course, referring to Jess and to myself, and not speaking about myself only in some strange third-person kind of reference. Thank you, Becca, Josh, Madi, and Lena, for being you.

I recently attended a book festival, and someone asked me what it felt like, or what my reaction was, to holding my first published book in my hands. My first book was published in 2015, and I'm fortunate to have quite a few books out now and even more on the horizon, but my answer was this: it was a surreal and wonderful feeling of accomplishment to know that I'd done what I set out to do when I was a ten-year-old with a dream—to hold in my hands a book that an agent, an editor, and you, the reader, felt was important enough, fun enough, good enough to invest in. And, I continued to say, that has never changed. I get that same feeling with every book. I am grateful for every opportunity, every reader, every book I publish. I am reminded of what I have managed to do and to not take any of this for granted. I am truly thankful for the ability and opportunity to put these books in your hands.

And speaking of book festivals, thank you so much to every organizer and volunteer of every book festival out there. Your hard work presents so many opportunities for us (the authors and illustrators) to meet old and new readers and share our art. Thank you, independent bookstore owners, for being the beating heart of the book world. There's so much more to this gig than shelf space and ISBNs.

Thank you to the teachers and librarians who celebrate reading, creativity, art, and writing in a STEM world. The classroom libraries you build, the book fairs, the authors and illustrators you bring in, and the school-wide reading nights may be more important to a young person than you may realize (but I'm betting I'm wrong—I'm betting you know just how important it is). And trust me when I say that you are making a difference. You may never know it, but you are. I might not ever learn the name of the fourth-grade teacher who changed my life. (We moved so much that it was somehow lost in the shuffle.) I will most likely never get a chance to thank her personally. But she saw in me what you see in some of your students, and her encouragement and belief in my potential put me on a trajectory that has me sitting here typing acknowledgments in this book. I am the fruit of your labor, teachers.

Lastly, I want to thank all of my fellow children's writers and illustrators. The art you produce, the work you do (from the books to the school visits to the signings and festivals), is a bright light in a sometimes dark world. We are the torchbearers. We bring the magic. I'm very proud to stand with you, helping children to learn, laugh, love, and discover. Yes, I know . . . discover does not start with an "l," and I missed a chance at nailing a four-word alliteration. But seriously, thank you. We all lift one another up and propel each other forward. Our kidlit community is pretty amazing.

Finally (even though I just previously said "lastly"), I'd like to thank every mom and dad who takes their kids to the bookstore and the library, who sends in their Scholastic Book Club money, who says yes to buying another book. I'm not thanking you for your money (although yes, I am thankful for that—it'd be rude not to say thanks for that, don't you think?)—I'm thanking you for feeding a child's hungry imagination, curious creativity, and insatiable appetite to explore new worlds and delve into new adventures. Thank you for saying yes when it's just as easy to say no.

Best to you all!

Joe